RUPERT
and the
Hidden Lake

Purnell

ISBN 0 361 05949 3
Copyright © 1983 Express Newspapers p.l.c.
Published 1983 by Purnell Books, Paulton,
Bristol, BS18 5LQ, Member of the BPCC Group.
Made and printed in Great Britain by Purnell and Sons
(Book Production) Limited, Paulton, Bristol,
Member of the BPCC Group.
Reprinted 1983

Rupert was feeling excited as he and his Mummy and Daddy prepared to leave for a holiday by the sea. The little bear followed his parents into the taxi which was to take them to the station.

"Won't it be lovely, Mummy," said the little bear. "I can't wait to paddle in the sea!"

At the station Mr Bear paid their fare and Rupert helped to carry their suitcases to the ticket office. They bought their tickets and had just walked on to the platform when the train drew in.

They found an empty compartment, and after a few minutes the train moved off. The

little bear looked with interest at all the places they passed on their journey.

"There's the sea!" cried Rupert some time later, and after clambering off the train with their luggage they walked the short distance from the station to their hotel.

"When we've unpacked our clothes may we go for a walk along the beach?" begged Rupert. "The tide is going out, and we could collect some shells."

"I think that's a good idea," said his mother.

The family quickly unpacked their clothes

and set off for the beach. Running along the sea-front, the little bear spied a telescope.

"Oh, Daddy, look!" he said. "Please may I try it?"

"Yes, of course," replied his father.

Rupert inserted a coin into the slot. Then he placed his eye to the telescope.

"I can see right across the bay," he said. "And I can see the lighthouse on that rocky headland. There's an odd-looking balcony and a sort of crane with a bell hanging from it at the top of the lighthouse. And I can see someone standing on the balcony!"

Suddenly the little bear gave a cry of astonishment.

"It's the Wise Old Goat! Whatever is he doing there?" shouted Rupert.

Mr Bear peered down the telescope. "It certainly looks like him," he said.

"Oh, Daddy, let's hire a boat and go and see him," pleaded Rupert. "I would love to know what he's doing in the lighthouse."

"Very well," he said. "I expect he'll be quite pleased to see some friends. We can hire a boat from the beach."

Mrs Bear decided to stay behind. "I think I'll sit on the beach and rest," she said. "I

feel quite tired after our walk. Don't be too
long," she called.

"Don't worry," replied the little bear.
"We shall be back quite soon."

Rupert followed his father on to the beach,
and they had soon hired a small motor boat
from a friendly boatman to carry them to the
lighthouse.

The little bear climbed into the front of the boat, and Mr Bear sat in the back to steer.

As Rupert and his father drew near to the lighthouse they saw the Wise Old Goat standing on the rocks waving to them.

"Ahoy there!" he greeted them. "This is a surprise!"

As soon as the visitors had landed, Rupert told the Wise Old Goat how they had seen him through the telescope.

Their friend led them up the steep steps into the lighthouse. "It's been empty for many years," he said, "and I decided to buy it. I am making a study of the sea, and this is an ideal spot from which to do it. Follow me and I'll show you my laboratory."

The little party climbed up to the top of the lighthouse into a round room filled with all manner of equipment.

"Here I have all I need for my study," he explained. "One of the things I am hoping to find is a rare sea-fern which I think may grow in these waters. I have designed the diving-bell outside to help me in my search. Come and look."

The group stepped out on to the balcony at the top of the lighthouse.

"Come over here," said the Wise Old Goat, pointing to the round, transparent object hanging from a crane on top of the lighthouse.

"This is my diving-bell," explained the

Wise Old Goat. "As you can see, it's very small. It's just big enough to take the Professor's dwarf servant. He's going to help me in my work. In fact, he is due to arrive today for the first descent to the sea-bed."

As he finished speaking the Wise Old Goat had to answer the telephone. He was gone for several minutes, and when he returned he looked quite upset.

"Oh dear," he said. "That was the Professor. His dwarf servant is ill and won't be able to come today after all. He may be in bed for at least a week. Now all my plans will have to be cancelled."

Rupert had a sudden idea. "Why couldn't I help you?" he suggested. "I'm not very big. Couldn't I help with your sea study?"

The Wise Old Goat smiled at the little bear. "Well, that would certainly help me a great deal," he said. "But what does your father think?"

Mr Bear thought carefully for several minutes. "I suppose you will come to no harm," he decided. "But you must promise to be very careful."

"Oh, thank you, Daddy," beamed Rupert. Turning excitedly to the Wise Old Goat he said, "When can we begin?"

"At once, if you are ready," said his friend. "The sea is very smooth, so we should waste no time."

The Wise Old Goat lowered the diving-bell on to the balcony by pulling some levers in the laboratory. Then he handed Rupert some glass jars.

"These are for specimens of the fern," said the Wise Old Goat.

As Rupert climbed into the diving-bell the

Wise Old Goat said, "You will find a small radio set on the side of the bell. I shall be able to give you instructions through that. Now, are you ready?"

"Yes," whispered Rupert, feeling rather nervous. "I think so."

The Wise Old Goat firmly closed the door of the diving-bell and returned to his laboratory. He pulled two huge levers on the wall and the crane hoisted the bell over the

balcony down towards the sea.

While the bell sank gently below the surface of the water the Wise Old Goat pressed another switch, which shone a

powerful light all around the bell.

Rupert gazed in astonishment at the sea-creatures all around him. As the diving-bell gently settled on the sea-bed he heard the Wise Old Goat's voice over the radio.

"Hullo, Rupert. Are you all right?"

"Oh yes," replied the little bear.

"Well now we can begin our study," said his friend. "If you hold those two levers on the ceiling you can move the bell wherever you want. I will release the diving-bell from

its cable, and you can start to look for the fern."

Holding on to the levers Rupert felt the bell lift up slightly from the sea-bed and begin to glide forward.

Suddenly, Rupert caught sight of the fern. Steering the bell closer, the little bear allowed the bell to sink on to the sea-bed once again, and then excitedly told the Wise Old Goat of his find.

"I know already," his friend laughed. "I have been following you on a little television screen here in my laboratory. Now, open the sliding door in the bottom of the bell and pick some fern."

Soon Rupert had completed his task, but as he was preparing to return to the surface he noticed that some fish were watching him.

"Oh dear," thought Rupert to himself. "They look very unhappy."

Then the little bear spied an eel wriggling into the bell through the sand underneath.

"Why do all the fish look so unhappy?" Rupert asked.

"It's because the sea is not as salty as it

used to be," explained the eel, "and it makes us very uncomfortable. The only answer is to open King Neptune's store of salt water in his lake on Brine Island. We have already sent a messenger to the King to ask for permission."

Rupert was very upset to hear of these
troubles, and promised to ask the Wise Old
Goat to help the sea-creatures. The eel
thanked Rupert and wriggled out of the
diving-bell on to the sandy sea-bed.

Rupert closed the hatch in the bottom of
the bell and, using the levers again, soon
guided the bell back to the cable. A press
of a switch automatically attached the cable
to the bell. Rupert felt the diving-bell
moving upwards, and it was soon hauled

back on to the balcony.

"Well done, Rupert!" said the Wise Old Goat, as he opened the door of the bell. "I'm delighted that you managed to find such fine specimens of the fern."

Rupert then told the Wise Old Goat about his conversation with the eel. When he had finished the story his friend said, "I couldn't quite hear what you were saying over the radio, but it sounded serious. Now we must try to help the sea-creatures."

The little party returned to the laboratory, and the Wise Old Goat produced a map.

"Look," he said. "This is Brine Island. It's not too far from here. This patch of blue in the centre is King Neptune's hidden lake. I

shall go there first thing in the morning and see if I can open the store of salt water and let it flood into the sea and make it saltier."

Rupert was staring excitedly at the map. "Oh, please may I go too?" he begged.

"Very well," said Mr Bear. "I'm sure our friend will look after you. And now I must be off to collect Mummy from the beach. I will come back tomorrow afternoon, Rupert."

"Goodbye!" cried Rupert.

After supper, the Wise Old Goat showed Rupert to a little bedroom. "I've left you some spare nightclothes," he said. "I will call you early in the morning."

As Rupert was dropping off to sleep he

was startled by a queer sound coming from
outside. The little bear pulled on his dressing
gown and climbed the winding stairs to the
balcony. To his amazement he saw some
flying fish circling around the lighthouse.
One of the fish flew right up to the little bear
and dropped a necklace into his hand.

"We are King Neptune's messengers,"
said the fish. "The King has asked us to give
you his emblem. If you show it to the
guardian of the lake, he will allow you to
open the lock gates. The King has given his

permission for the salt water to be released into the ocean.''

Rupert was delighted. "Oh, thank you," he said. In the morning, Rupert told the Wise Old Goat about the flying fish.

"I think you should wear the necklace around your neck, Rupert," advised his

friend. "Then the guardian of the hidden lake will know that we are not enemies. And now I will show you our flying machines."

The Wise Old Goat disappeared into his laboratory and returned a few minutes later dressed in a flying suit, with a machine strapped to his back. He handed Rupert a smaller machine and some goggles.

"We shall reach Brine Island in no time with these."

On the balcony the Wise Old Goat strapped the machine to Rupert's back, and told him how to use it.

"There are two arm-rests with a cross-bar between them," he said. "All you do is twist the bar one way to go slowly, and the other way to go fast. It's very simple."

The pair started up the machines and quickly soared into the sky.

"I feel like a bird!" cried Rupert.

They flew higher and higher, leaving land far behind, and soon Rupert could see nothing but sea beneath him. At length the Wise Old Goat shouted, "Look! There's land ahead! That should be Brine Island."

As the pair flew on the little bear saw the outline of a desolate island.

The Wise Old Goat flew towards the centre of the island, and then began to descend. "Look below you, Rupert," he shouted. "There's King Neptune's lake!"

Beneath him Rupert spied an enormous stretch of water. Following the Wise Old Goat, the little bear flew down towards the surface, and the pair landed on a rocky ledge.

Turning to Rupert the Wise Old Goat said, "Throw a few stones into the water. If this is the hidden lake they won't sink because the water is so salty."

Rupert picked up a handful of stones and threw them into the lake. To his astonishment they remained on the surface. "We must have found the right place!" he laughed.

"Now we must find the lock gates which hold the water in the lake. I think that is the direction we must take," said the Wise Old Goat, pointing towards one end of the lake.

The pair set off on their journey. The way was very rocky, but at length they saw a great wooden barrier ahead of them.

"That must be the lock gates," cried the Wise Old Goat.

As the pair neared the gates Rupert noticed a curious disturbance in the water.

"What's that, I wonder?" he muttered.

The Wise Old Goat peered closely at the spot, and as he did so the disturbance grew greater, and the water began to churn and froth.

"There's something in the water, Rupert," cried the Wise Old Goat. "Quickly, fly up into the air again. We'll be safe from danger there."

The Wise Old Goat quickly started his flying machine and was soon hovering in the air above his little friend.

The little bear turned on his machine, but found to his horror that it would not start. It made a sputtering noise and then stopped. Then a great figure rose out of the water in front of him. It had a huge shaggy head, and

a tail shaped like a fish.

Trembling with fear Rupert gasped, "It's a merman. I do hope he doesn't hurt me!"

He wanted to run away, but before he

could move the merman caught his leg.

"I am the guardian of the lake," the merman thundered angrily. "Who are you that you dare to come to this island?"

As Rupert anxiously began to explain, the Wise Old Goat flew down to the ground beside him.

"Leave my young friend alone," the Wise Old Goat ordered the huge merman. "Can't you see that he is wearing your King's emblem? King Neptune has given permission for us to open the lock gates and let the salt water run into a part of the ocean where the sea-creatures are in desperate need of it."

The merman's anger died down as he heard the story. "That is indeed King Neptune's emblem you are wearing," he said. "This means that my work here has ended. Many years ago the King asked me to guard the hidden lake until its salt water was needed to replenish the ocean. Now my task

is completed and I can return to my home in the ocean. I will open the lock gates for you," and the huge figure swam across the barrier.

The two friends gazed in astonishment as the merman pulled on the enormous wooden beams. Slowly the gates moved apart, and the salt water from the lake began gushing forth

on its journey to the ocean. The merman rose up in the water once again, and his great voice boomed across to Rupert and the Wise Old Goat.

"Goodbye, my friends. I am returning to my ocean home." His great body disappeared into the foaming water and he swam out towards the sea.

As the pair watched the merman swimming strongly away, the Wise Old Goat said, "Now we must devise a way of getting you home, little bear. Your flying machine is beyond repair, and mine isn't powerful enough to carry both of us."

He thought for a few moments and then had an idea. "I know just the thing," he smiled. "Would you collect some large leaves for me while I find some springy branches?"

Rupert did as he was asked while the Wise Old Goat found some branches and lashed them together to make the framework of a shallow bowl.

The little bear watched, mystified, as his friend covered the branches with leaves and laced them together with creepers.

"Now you have a little boat to travel back in, Rupert!" smiled the Wise Old Goat. "It's small, but quite strong enough to take a small person like you."

Rupert and his friend carried the boat to the water beyond the opened lock gates. "As soon as we reach the sea, I will take you in tow," promised the Wise Old Goat. "But until then I shall fly above you, and make sure that you don't come to any harm."

Rupert felt quite anxious, but climbed into the craft. The Wise Old Goat pushed him out into the current.

Reaching the middle of the current from the lake, the little craft was tossed about in the surging waters. Rupert crouched on the bottom of the craft, clutching the sides of the boat to prevent himself from being thrown overboard. He looked up and saw the Wise Old Goat hovering above him.

"Hold on tight, my friend," he called. "The waters will be calmer when we reach the ocean."

At that moment the flood swept down a narrow valley, and Rupert felt the spray from the tossing waves fall on to his back.

"Hold on tightly, Rupert," the Wise Old Goat called above him. "There are some dangerous rapids ahead."

Rupert clutched the sides of the craft even

more tightly as it was swept through frothing waves and swirling currents. Just as he felt he could hold on no longer the waters suddenly became calm. Peering over the edge of the craft, Rupert saw the valley behind him and the great ocean ahead.

"Oh, thank goodness," he cried in relief. "We've reached the sea!"

"Yes," called the Wise Old Goat. "You were very brave, little bear. Now I can take you in tow."

Hovering in the air, the Wise Old Goat lowered a rope to Rupert. The little bear fastened it securely to the front of the craft, and his friend increased the speed of his flying machine.

The sun was setting as the pair caught sight of the lighthouse in the distance. "There it is," sighed Rupert happily. "I do hope Daddy isn't worried about me."

Nearing the rocks on which the lighthouse stood, Rupert spied a motor boat in the distance.

"There's Daddy," he shouted. "Hooray! He's only just come to fetch me!"

The Wise Old Goat flew down on to the rocks and pulled Rupert's little craft into the edge. The pair waited for Mr Bear, and then helped him to clamber ashore. As he tied the boat securely to a rock, Rupert told Mr Bear all about their adventures.

"Well, it has all been worthwhile," smiled
Mr Bear. "The currents in the ocean will
soon spread the salt from the hidden lake,
and the sea-creatures will be happy again.
What a very good start to our holiday!"

As Mr Bear was speaking two dolphins
leapt up from the water around the rocks.

"Why, I do believe they are thanking us,"
laughed Rupert. "Look how happy they
seem!"

It was time for Rupert and Mr Bear to
return to shore. "Mummy will wonder
where we both are," said Mr Bear.

Clambering back into the motor boat they
waved goodbye to the Wise Old Goat, who
was standing by the lighthouse.

"Goodbye," he called. "I will see you back
in Nutwood!"

As they left the lighthouse far behind, Mr Bear noticed some flying fish in the distance.

"That's odd," he murmured. "They seem to be coming this way."

Just then Rupert remembered the emblem he was still wearing around his neck. He gave a cry. "Of course! They have come to collect King Neptune's necklace!"

As the fish drew nearer to the boat, Rupert removed the necklace and threw it high into the air. One of the fish caught it in his mouth, and then the whole group turned and flew towards the horizon.

When they reached the shore Rupert recounted his adventures to the boatman who stared in disbelief.

"Well, that beats the tallest fisherman's story I've ever heard!" he laughed.